FOSSIL
FOLLIES!

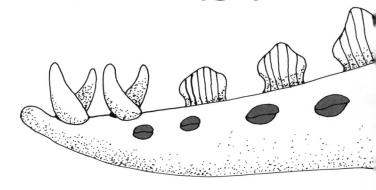

Lerner Publications Company · Minneapolis

FOSSIL FOLLIES!

jokes about dinosaurs

by Rick & Ann Walton / pictures by Joan Hanson

This book is available in two editions:
Library binding by Lerner Publications Company
Soft cover by First Avenue Editions
241 First Avenue North
Minneapolis, Minnesota 55401

Library of Congress Cataloging-in-Publication Data

Walton, Rick.
    Fossil follies!: jokes about dinosaurs / by Rick & Ann Walton;
pictures by Joan Hanson.
    p. cm. — (Make me laugh!)
    Summary: A collection of jokes about dinosaurs including
"What do you get if you feed your nodosaurus gunpowder?
Dino-mite."
    ISBN 0-8225-0974-1 (lib. bdg.)
    ISBN 0-8225-9560-5 (pbk.)
    1. Dinosaurs—Juvenile humor. 2. Wit and humor, Juvenile.
I. Walton, Ann, 1963-   II. Hanson, Joan, ill. III. Title.
IV. Series.
PN6231.D65W35   1988   88-23007
818'.5402-dc19   CIP
                                                              AC

Manufactured in the United States of America

    2   3   4   5   6   7   8   9   10   98   97   96   95   94   93   92   91   90   89

Q: What should you do if you find a dinosaur
in your bathtub?

A: Pull the plug and wash her down the drain.

Q: What do you get if you flush a triceratops down the toilet?

A: A dino-sewer.

Q: What would you call it if it rained dinosaurs over your town?

A: A disaster.

Q: Why don't you see dinosaurs in zoos?

A: Because they hide behind the trees.

Q: How do you make a ceratosaurus cross?

A: Show him where the bridge is and tug on his leash.

Q: Why don't polite dinosaurs jump into the ocean?

A: Because they don't like to make waves.

Q: If you see an allosaurus on your front lawn, why is it safest to stay indoors?

A: Because an allosaurus will only eat you out of house and home.

Q: What bed should a diplodocus sleep in when he comes to visit you?

A: The flower bed.

Q: What kind of dinosaur do rabbits like to eat?

A: Tri-carrot-tops.

Q: Why do dinosaurs hate walking through forests?

A: Because the trees tickle their feet.

Q: How do you make a dinosaur roll?
A: Mix together 10,000 pounds of flour, 500 gallons of water, and one dinosaur. Bake for 30 minutes at 350°.

Q: How do you cook petrified eggs?
A: Hard boil them.

Q: What do you get if you break a brachio-saurus egg?
A: A really big omelet.

Q: Why do dinosaurs like to eat snowmen?
A: They melt in their mouths.

Q: What do you get if you feed your nodo-saurus gunpowder?

A: Dino-mite.

Q: What does a ceratosaurus do when she gets a toothache?

A: She eats a dentist.

Q: Why did the allosaurus eat Fort Knox?

A: His dentist told him he needed a gold filling.

Q: What do you get if a tyrannosaurus bites you?

A: A dino-sore.

Q: What do you get when you put an opisthocoelicaudia in a hypodermic needle?

A: A big shot.

Q: Why did the dinosaurs die?
A: Because they didn't look both ways before crossing the street.

Q: Why is it impossible to wake a dinosaur?
A: Because dinosaurs are dead to the world.

Q: Did dinosaurs ever die indoors?
A: No, they died out.

Q: Why did dinosaurs enjoy the day they died?
A: Because it was the living end.

Q: How do dinosaurs make ends meet?
A: They put their tails in their mouths.

Q: Why should you keep money away from a camarasaurus?

A: Because a camarasaurus likes to eat green things.

Q: Why is having no money like having an iguanodon sit on you?

A: Because either way you're flat broke.

Q: What did the deinonychus say when he got a horse for his birthday?

A: "Look, a gift horse in the mouth!"

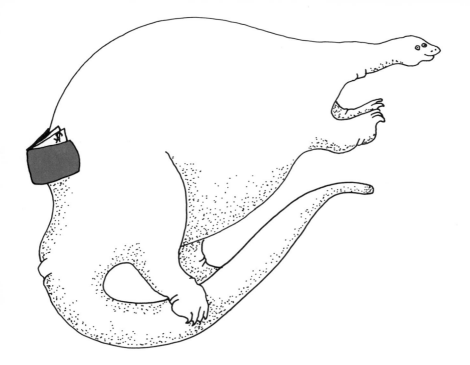

Q: Why shouldn't you keep an apatosaurus in your wallet?

A: Because then you wouldn't have room for your credit cards.

Q: Why shouldn't you let a tyrannosaurus drive your car?

A: Because the tyrannosaurus wrecks.

Q: What kind of plants would dinosaurs eat today?

A: Automobile plants.

Q: What do you call a petrified tyranno-saurus rex?

A: Tyrannosaurus rocks.

Q: How did prehistoric animals advertise?
A: On sign-osaurs.

Q: When is it time to end your friendship with a baryonyx?

A: When she invites you for dinner.

Q: What does a tyrannosaurus rex have to eat at a restaurant?

A: Waiters.

Q: Why are there no photographs of dinosaurs?

A: Because dinosaurs are camera shy.

Q: What do you call a hundred dancing dinosaurs?

A: An earthquake.

Q: What's the hardest thing about teaching a dinosaur to dance?

A: Finding a tutu to fit him.

Q: Why does an allosaurus make a poor after-dinner speaker?

A: Because after the allosaurus has dinner, there's no one to speak to.

Q: What do you get when you cross a stegosaurus with a boomerang?

A: An extinct creature that comes back to life.

Q: What do you call dinosaurs standing on their heads?

A: Tall tails.

Q: Why did the tyrannosaurus eat the team of acrobats?

A: She wanted a well-balanced meal.

Q: What do you get when you cross an apato-saurus with a poker game?

A: A big deal.

Q: Where do dinosaurs like to jog?

A: On runways.

Q: Which dinosaur is the fastest?

A: The pronto-saurus.

Q: Why aren't dinosaurs allowed to play professional football?

A: Because they keep crushing the passer.

Q: Why do volleyball players hate playing with a stegosaurus?

A: Because a stegosaurus always spikes the ball.

Q: What do you get when you cross a dinosaur with a dictionary?

A: Big words.

Q: Why is it fun to listen to an ankylosaurus?

A: Because an ankylosaurus has quite a tail.

Q: Why shouldn't you tell secrets to a dinosaur?

A: Because dinosaurs have big mouths.

Q: How do you unlock the mystery of dinosaur bones?

A: With a skeleton key.

Q: How can you tell a dinosaur in disguise?
A: His false nose is six feet long.

Q: What flies through the air and does mean things to dogs and cats?

A: A terrible-dactyl.

Q: Why can you trust a dinosaur to help you in your hour of need?

A: Because dinosaurs are big-hearted.

Q: How do you make friends with a diplodocus?

A: You put the friends together while the diplodocus reads the instructions.

Q: What did your parents do when you brought the dinosaur home to live with you?

A: They raised the roof.

ABOUT THE ARTIST

JOAN HANSON lives with her husband and two sons in Afton, Minnesota. Her distinctive, deliberately whimsical pen-and-ink drawings have illustrated more than 30 children's books. Hanson is also an accomplished weaver. A graduate of Carleton College, Hanson enjoys tennis, skiing, sailing, reading, traveling, and walking in the woods surrounding her home.

ABOUT THE AUTHORS

RICK AND ANN WALTON love to read, travel, play guitar, study foreign languages, and write for children. Rick also collects books and writes music while Ann knits and does origami. They are both graduates of Brigham Young University and live in Kearns, Utah, where Rick teaches sixth grade.

Make Me Laugh!